Learn FRENCH Through Fairy Tales

Beauty and the Beast

Book Design & Production: Slangman Kids *(a division of Slangman Inc. and Slangman Publishing)*

Copy Editor: Julie Bobrick
Illustrated by: "Migs!" Sandoval
Translator: "Slangman" David Burke
Proofreader: Emmanuelle Rousseaux

Copyright © 2006 by David Burke

Published by: Slangman Kids *(a division of Slangman Inc. and Slangman Publishing)* 12206 Hillslope Street, Studio City, CA 91604 • USA • Toll Free Telephone from USA: 1-877-SLANGMAN (1-877-752-6462) • From outside the USA: 1-818-SLANGMAN (1-818-752-6462) • Worldwide Fax 1-413-647-1589 • Email: info@slangman.com • Website: www.slangman.com

Slangman is a trademark of David Burke. All rights reserved. Reproduction or translation of any part of this work beyond that permitted by section 107 or 108 of the 1976 United States Copyright Act without the permission of the copyright owner is unlawful. Requests for permission or further information should be addressed to the Permissions Department, Slangman Publishing. This publication is designed to provide accurate and authoritative information in regard to the subject matter covered. The persons, entities and events in this book are fictitious. Any similarities with actual persons or entities, past and present, are purely coincidental.

"Migs!" Sandoval ✷ our illustrator ✷

Miguel *"Migs!"* Sandoval has been drawing cartoons since the age of 6 and has worked on numerous national commercials and movies as a sculptor, model builder, and illustrator. He was born in Los Angeles and was raised in a bilingual household, speaking English and Spanish. He currently lives in San Francisco where he is working on his new comic book series!

ISBN10: 1891888-870
ISBN13: 978189888-878
Printed in the U.S.A.
10 9 8 7 6 5 4 3 2 1

Order Form

Preview chapters & shop online!
www.slangman.com

SHIP TO: _____

_____

_____

_____

Contact/Phone/Email: _____

SHIPPING

Domestic Orders

SURFACE MAIL
(Delivery time 5-7 business days).
Add $5 shipping/handling for the first item, $1.50 for each additional item.

RUSH SERVICE
Available at extra charge. Contact us for details.

International Orders

SURFACE MAIL
(Delivery time 6-8 weeks).
Add $6 shipping/handling for the first item, $2 for each additional item. Note that shipping to some countries may be more expensive. Contact us for details.

AIRMAIL (approx. 3-5 business days)
Available at extra charge. Contact us for details.

Method of Payment (Check one):

☐ Personal Check or Money Order
(Must be in U.S. funds and drawn on a U.S. bank.)

☐ VISA ☐ Master Card ☐ Discover ☐ American Express ☐ JCB

Credit Card Number

Signature | Expiration Date

QTY	ISBN-13	TITLE	PRICE	LEVEL	TOTAL COST
English to CHINESE (Mandarin)					
	9781891888-793	Cinderella	$14.95	1	
	9781891888-854	Goldilocks	$14.95	2	
	9781891888-915	Beauty and the Beast	$14.95	3	
English to FRENCH					
	9781891888-755	Cinderella	$14.95	1	
	9781891888-816	Goldilocks	$14.95	2	
	9781891888-878	Beauty and the Beast	$14.95	3	
English to GERMAN					
	9781891888-762	Cinderella	$14.95	1	
	9781891888-830	Goldilocks	$14.95	2	
	9781891888-885	Beauty and the Beast	$14.95	3	
English to HEBREW					
	9781891888-922	Cinderella	$14.95	1	
	9781891888-939	Goldilocks	$14.95	2	
	9781891888-946	Beauty and the Beast	$14.95	3	
English to ITALIAN					
	9781891888-779	Cinderella	$14.95	1	
	9781891888-823	Goldilocks	$14.95	2	
	9781891888-892	Beauty and the Beast	$14.95	3	
English to JAPANESE					
	9781891888-786	Cinderella	$14.95	1	
	9781891888-847	Goldilocks	$14.95	2	
	9781891888-908	Beauty and the Beast	$14.95	3	
English to SPANISH					
	9781891888-748	Cinderella	$14.95	1	
	9781891888-809	Goldilocks	$14.95	2	
	9781891888-861	Beauty and the Beast	$14.95	3	
Japanese to ENGLISH 絵本で えいご を学ぼう						
	9781891888-038	Cinderella	$14.95	1	
	9781891888-045	Goldilocks	$14.95	2	
	9781891888-052	Beauty and the Beast	$14.95	3	
Korean to ENGLISH 동화를 통한 ENGLISH 배우기					
	9781891888-076	Cinderella	$14.95	1	
	9781891888-106	Goldilocks	$14.95	2	
	9781891888-113	Beauty and the Beast	$14.95	3	
Spanish to ENGLISH Aprende INGLÉS con cuentos de hadas					
	9781891888-953	Cinderella	$14.95	1	
	9781891888-960	Goldilocks	$14.95	2	
	9781891888-977	Beauty and the Beast	$14.95	3	

Total for Merchandise

Sales Tax (California residents only add applicable sales tax)

Shipping (See left)

ORDER GRAND TOTAL

Prices subject to change

SLANGMAN® KIDS

(a division of Slangman Publishing)

** TO PLACE AN ORDER - CALL, FAX, OR EMAIL: **

Phone: 1-818-752-6462 • Fax: 1-413-647-1589
Email: info@slangman.com • Web: www.slangman.com
12206 Hillslope Street • Studio City, CA 91604

(FORM 071606)

Dedication

The entire "Foreign Language Through Fairy Tales" series is dedicated to all the children of the world.

It is through their understanding, appreciation, and celebration of our differences that the world will become a better and safer place for us all.

One thing to remember...

The words in *green italics* throughout this fairy tale are words you've already learned in previous levels! Do you still remember what they mean?

1

beaucoup

Once upon a time, there was a *papa* who had an eldest *fille* named Julie, a middle *fille* named Tessa, and a youngest *fille* named Belle. He loved them very much. While getting ready to take a long (trip), he asked each *fille*, "What can I bring you from my **voyage**?" "I'd like a (ring) to wear on my finger," said Julie. "I'd like a (necklace) to wear around my neck." said Tessa.

voyage

bague

collier

3

S'il vous plaît ← But Belle, who was the most **belle** of all said, "⟨Please⟩. I don't want a **bague** to wear on my finger or a **collier** to wear around my neck.

rose ← All I want is a ⟨rose⟩." He replied, "You shall

each receive your gift." "Oh, *merci!*" said each *fille*. Then their *papa* mounted his horse, and they shouted "Have a good **voyage**, *papa*! **Bon voyage**! We will miss you **beaucoup**!"

cadeau
cheval
bon

5

As he rode off, each **fille** shouted again, "**Au revoir, Papa! Au revoir!**" until he was out of sight. Days later, it was time for him to return. So he first stopped to buy a **bague** for his eldest *fille* to wear on her finger, a **collier** for his second *fille* to wear around her neck, but he waited to get closer to his *maison* to look for a garden where he could find a **rose** for

jardin

7

Belle. After a few hours, he saw a magnificent **jardin**. He got off his **cheval**, walked into the **jardin** and picked a **rose** that was the most *belle* he'd ever seen. At that *moment*, the *porte* to the *maison* opened and a *grande* [beast] came out and ran toward him. "Who stole a **rose** from my **jardin**?" exploded the *grande* **bête**. "**S'il vous plaît**, [Sir]!" said the *papa*.

→ **bête**

→ **monsieur**

8

9

"**S'il vous plaît**, don't hurt me, **monsieur**. I promised my *fille*, Belle, I'd bring her a **rose** as a **cadeau** after my long **voyage**. It was just ONE **rose** from your **jardin**!" "It's still stealing!" said the **grande** **bête**. "I will spare your life if you bring me the **fille** you speak of by noon in six days. Here she will live the rest of her life." Naturally, the

midi
six

11

papa was very *triste* by this request, but he promised he'd return with Belle at **midi** in **six** days. As he arrived home, each *fille* rushed out to greet him. He gave them each the **cadeau** they'd asked for. Each *fille* was very *heureuse* and shouted, "*Merci* **beaucoup**, *papa. Merci!*" "*De rien!*" he replied. But he was still *triste* because he had to tell Belle

13

je t'amie

about the promise he'd made with the **grande bête**. "Belle, I love you **beaucoup** and want you to be **heureuse**. But I must tell you what I have done…" Her **papa** went on to explain what had happened that day and about the promise he had made. He warned her about how ugly the **grande bête** was, but Belle felt responsible because the **rose** was a **cadeau**

moche

15

she'd requested. So, she agreed to go. **Six** days passed quickly and it was time to leave. Each *fille* was very *triste* to say *au revoir* to Belle, but they understood that she had no choice.

So, Belle and her *papa* mounted the **cheval** and rode off. They arrived at exactly **midi** as instructed. Belle and her *papa* got off the **cheval** and approached the *maison* of the *grande* **bête**.

17

Bonjour ← The **porte** opened slowly and they walked in. "Hello!" said the **papa**. "**Bonjour**!" But there was no answer. As they walked in, they saw a **grande table** in the middle of the **cuisine** filled with food.

It looked like someone was having a **grande fête**! Just then they heard a deep voice say, "**Bonjour**. This lunch is especially for you. **S'il vous plaît**, enjoy!" Not wanting to be impolite, they began

déjeuner

19

quatre

cinq

eating the magnificent **déjeuner** before them. And so many desserts! Belle was so excited and already busily counting them. "...four, five, **six**. **Six** different, wonderful desserts!

She counted them again just to make sure, "*Un*, *deux*, *trois*, **quatre**, **cinq**, **six**! It was true! **Six** delicious desserts all for them! They had never seen a more wonderful

21

déjeuner in their lives! Suddenly, they heard footsteps approaching. There he was – the **grande bête** himself. Indeed, he was truly **moche**. Scared, Belle said, "**Bonjour**,

monsieur and **merci** for the delicious *déjeuner*." "*De rien*," replied the *grande bête*. He seemed very kind toward Belle. Her *papa* was permitted to come visit her every week

gentil

23

which made her very *heureuse*. He gave Belle a kiss on the cheek, mounted his **cheval** and said, "*Au revoir*, Belle. **Je t'aime beaucoup**!" and rode off back to his *maison*. At that *moment*, the **grande bête** turned toward Belle and said, "**S'il vous plaît**. What's mine is yours. I will return every day at **midi** to see you." He then quickly ran off, leaving Belle alone.

25

Because he was so **gentil** toward her, Belle was no longer afraid, and was even *heureuse* when he came to visit at **midi**. Every day, they laughed more and more and enjoyed sharing stories with each other. But one day, the **grande bête** didn't arrive at **midi** as usual, so Belle went to look for him. She walked outside into the

27

jardin and there he was lying on the ground lifeless. Belle cried, "Oh, why did you have to die? **Je t'aime! Je t'aime beaucoup!**" She gave him a kiss on the cheek and

suddenly, right before her eyes, he awoke
and was transformed into a **beau prince**!
He explained to her that an evil magician
had changed him into a **grande bête** and

only the kiss of a *fille* who was truly in love with him, and the words "**Je t'aime**" could change him back. The next day at **midi**, Belle became his *épouse*, and they all lived happily ever after.